What a Naughty Bird!

Sean Taylor & Dan Widdowson

templar publishing

I'm sorry, but when you're a bird,
There's something you've just got to do.

What a Naughty Bird!

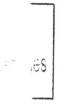

For Liam, Lua and Lowen - ST
For mum and dad and every art teacher
I've ever had - DW

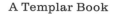

A Templar Book

First published in the UK in 2015 by Templar Publishing,
an imprint of the Bonnier Company Limited,
Deepdene Lodge, Deepdene Avenue,
Dorking, Surrey, RH5 4AT, UK

www.templarco.co.uk

ISBN: 978-1-78370-246-6 (Hardback)
ISBN: 978-1-78370-348-7 (Softback)

Edited by Zanna Davidson
Designed by Genevieve Webster

Printed in China

Fly to a farm, spot a **big** bull . . .

. . . and **splat** him with some **poo!**

What
a naughty
bird!

Once I was over in Africa,
And I thought it might be a laugh,

To do a **poo** on an elephant . . .

. . . and I did (though it gave me a bath)!

What a naughty bird!

Another time up in the mountains,

I made best friends with a rabbit.

When I did a **big poo** right on the nose,

Of a wolf who was trying to grab it!

What a naughty bird!

I can **splash** the middle of a puddle,

I can **hit** the last leaf on a tree!

I even splattered a great white shark
When he stuck his head out of the sea!

What a naughty bird!

And **pooing** on people is best!
Once from high up on a wall . . .
I got two policemen, a builder, a teacher,
Three children and their ball!

What a naughty bird!

But I shouldn't have **pooed** on a bear,

The bear didn't like it you see.

And the problem is that I forgot . . .

A **bear** can climb a tree . . .

The
end